Man About the House

C A Plaisted

A & C Black • London

The rights of C A Plaisted and Nelson Evergreen to be identified
as the author and illustrator of this work have been asserted by them
in accordance with the Copyrights, Designs and Patents Act 1988.

ISBN 978-1-4081-5654-4

A CIP catalogue for this book is available from the British Library.

This book is produced using paper that is made from wood
grown in managed, sustainable forests. It is natural, renewable
and recyclable. The logging and manufacturing processes conform
to the environmental regulations of the country of origin.

Printed by CPI Group (UK), Croydon, CR0 4YY.

recommended by

www.catchup.org

Catch Up is a not-for-profit charity
which aims to address the problem of
underachievement that has its roots in
literacy and numeracy difficulties.

Contents

Chapter 1

A Man's Work

"I told you I am not going!"

That was Fliss. My sister. Fliss is in a strop. Nothing new there, then.

"That's so not fair!" I say. "I've got to go. So why don't you?"

We are talking about going to Dad's.

We go to him at weekends. Well, we are meant to see him at weekends. I do. But Fliss always gets out of it.

"I can't go!" Fliss yells. "I've got my Saturday job. And my GCSE stuff. I'm busy!"

We are washing up. I have to dry. Fliss won't let me wash.

"Err – gross! Like I'd trust you to get stuff clean," she says. "You can't even wash yourself."

"You really rate yourself, don't you?" I say.

Fliss screams back at me.

"Give it a rest, you two!" cries Mum.

But we don't listen. We go on. Well, Fliss goes on. I want to ignore her. But she's in my face and I can't ignore her.

Then Grandpa turns up. Grandpa is my mum's dad.

"Hi, Grandpa!" Fliss says. She's all smiles now. The perfect princess. Not at all like she's just been with me.

They talk about what she's been up to at school and stuff. Then Grandpa comes over to me.

"Hi," I say, wiping another plate.

"Glad to see you helping your mum," Grandpa says. "You are the man about the house after all, Jeza."

"'Course," I say.

But inside I wonder why Grandpa always has to say that. That stuff about me being the 'man'. What's that all about?

He never goes on about Fliss helping.

"Mum says the shower is not draining right," Grandpa says. "Shall we see if we can sort it?"

It's true. The water doesn't go down the plughole. It stays in a pool around your ankles. It's gross.

"Shall we do it now?" Grandpa asks.

But there's a film I really want to watch on the telly. And it starts in a minute.

"Why can't Fliss do it?" I wail.

"Jeza!" Mum snaps at me. "Don't talk to Grandpa like that!"

My cheeks go red. Fliss giggles. Like she's won one over on me.

"OK, OK!" I say, flinging the wet tea towel on the table. "What do you want me to do?"

"Come on, mate," says Grandpa. He puts his hand on my shoulder. "Let's get my tool bag."

So we go to the bathroom.

The shower is all manky. The water has gone down now. But the tray is covered in soap scum. And hair. And weird gunk. I don't even want to know what *that* is.

"I expect the plughole is a bit blocked," Grandpa says.

I look at my watch. The film is starting.

Grandpa is scratching his chin.

"So what do we do?" I ask.

"Pull the plug cover out," Grandpa says.

He leans down to the shower tray. He pokes around. Pop!

"There!" says Grandpa. "Got it!"

I move from foot to foot. *Get on with it!* I think. *I want to see the film.*

Grandpa is poking around in the plughole.

"It's no good," he says. "I can't do it. My fingers are too big. You need to do it. Have a poke around. Something's blocking it. Hair, I reckon."

"Me?" I say. I don't want to poke around in hair and shower slime! "Why can't Mum do it?" I grumble. "Or Fliss?"

"It's a man's job, mate," Grandpa says.

I glare at Grandpa.

"Come on, Jeza," Grandpa says.

So I bend down. I stick my fingers in the drain.

"Oh, gross!" I say. It's all slimy! And cold! It smells, too. I can feel a soft lump of mush in my fingers. I scoop it out.

"It smells like puke!" I say.

In my hand is a lump of grey slime. There is a huge ball of hair in the middle.

I gag. It really smells.

"Well done, Jeza," Grandpa says. "Looks like you've cleared it."

I gag again. The smell is truly awful.

Mum comes in.

"Jeza's sorted it." Grandpa grins. "It was blocked with hair."

"Yes," I say. "Look! Long, black hair. Fliss's hair!"

I chuck the gunk in the bin and wash my hands.

"That was *rank*," I say. "Why should I have to clean up after Fliss all the time?"

"Plumbing is a man's job," Grandpa says. "And you sorted it for your mum."

"Huh!" I say. "Whatever."

And I storm out of the bathroom. I'm going to watch the film.

Chapter 2

The Visit

It's Saturday morning. I am on the bus. Fliss isn't with me. Surprise, surprise.

I am on my way to Dad's. Well – Dad and Ava's. Ava is Dad's girlfriend. They've got a baby. She's called Lulu.

Lulu is my half-sister. So now I've got two sisters. How unfair is that?

My mum and dad split up when I was a baby. I can't remember Dad living with us.

I don't have a bedroom at Dad's. The house is too small. I have to sleep in a kind of cupboard. Lulu has a much bigger room. But at least I don't have to share with a baby.

Ava is kind of OK. But she's always asking me if I am all right. Do I want something to eat? What am I doing? What am I watching? Stuff like that. *All* the time. It gets on my nerves.

I wish she would just leave me alone.

Anyway, I get off the bus. I walk to Dad's and I ring the bell. I don't even have a key.

But this house isn't my home. This is a house I visit.

"Hiya, Jeza!" says Ava.

"Jeza! Jeza!" says Lulu, grabbing my knees.

Lulu won't let go of me. She giggles as I try to walk with her stuck to my legs.

"Hi, Jeza," says Dad. "You alright?"

"Yeah," I say.

"And how's Fliss?" Dad goes on.

"OK," I say.

"So what's Fliss up to today?" says Dad.

"Work and stuff," I say. "You know."

"She hasn't come here for ages," Dad says.

But I have, I think. *I come every week.*

Dad goes on and on about Fliss.

What's she doing at school? Has she got a boyfriend?

"Who cares?" I say. "If you're so interested, why don't you ask her?"

"There's no need to be like that," Dad says.

Ava stares at me. Then at Dad. Then she says it's time for lunch.

We talk about stuff at school as we eat. Dad asks questions. But when I answer, he's looking at Lulu. He isn't really listening.

"Isn't she cute?" Dad keeps saying. Lulu has food round her face.

"Sure," I say. But I don't think he hears.

"What shall we do this afternoon?" Dad asks.

"There's a great film just out," I say.

And I tell him and Ava about the film my mates have been to, with these really cool fighting aliens. I *really* want to see it.

"But it's not one Lulu can go to see," says Dad.

So we go to some stupid cartoon film about penguins instead. No one asks me if I want to see it.

I suppose the film is OK. Kind of funny. But it isn't cool. And I won't tell my mates about it.

We spend the evening watching some stupid talent show on telly. It's so lame. I can't play any PS3 games or anything at Dad's. He hasn't got any. I can't even search the net without Lulu getting in the way.

So I play Duplo with Lulu instead. I'm glad my mates at school can't see me.

Playing Duplo with Lulu is a big mistake. I end up spending all day on Sunday making Duplo towers for Lulu to knock down.

Lulu giggles as the towers fall down. It makes me laugh too.

"She loves you playing with her," says Ava.

I stop giggling.

Yeah, I think. *But I don't love playing with some baby.*

On Sunday afternoon, I go home. When I get in, Fliss says I need a shower because I smell.

Cow!

Chapter 3

Football and Fights

It's break time on Monday and I'm kicking a football around with my mates Rory, Kismat and Callum. We've always been at school together.

"I went to a match with my dad on Saturday," says Rory.

Rory lives with his mum like me. He's got a stepdad who's OK. But his real dad is always taking him to places.

"Where did you go?" asks Callum.

It turns out that he only went to see Arsenal!

"Get out of here!" says Kismat. "That's not fair. I had to help my dad paint the kitchen."

"I had to go to my gran's house for some massive family party," says Callum. "So boring! What about you, Jeza?"

I groan. "Just hanging about at Dad's. Come on – let's play."

There's no way I'm going to tell them that I watched a film about penguins and played Duplo with a baby.

I kick the ball towards Kismat.

My mates may think they had a boring weekend. But I wish I did normal stuff like that with my dad. I can't even remember the last time I saw my dad on my own.

Fliss moans at me all week. "You are so disgusting!" she goes.

"Get out of my face!" I yell back at her. "You're not in charge! You act like you are my mum."

Mum tells us both to stop it. She tells Fliss to say nothing if she can't say anything nice.

"Oh, that's right," says Fliss. "Stick up for him."

Mum sighs. She takes me to one side and says, "Try to ignore her. Don't rise to her bait."

"Why don't you tell Fliss not to annoy me, then?" I yell.

Mum slumps down on a chair. And I run upstairs. Loudly.

Bang! I slam my bedroom door.

Up in my room, I feel hot with anger. I don't know what to do. I pace up and down. I see my PS3 games on the shelf. I grab them and chuck them on the floor. Then I kick at them as hard as I can. One of the boxes lands near the wall. I stamp on it again and again, until it smashes into pieces.

I did that. I broke it. And I've no idea why.

Chapter 4

Saturday Again

Fliss is annoying all week. She never stops. So I am glad to go to Dad's on Saturday. When I get there, I ask if we can play football.

"Good idea, mate," Dad says.

Result! I think.

But then he puts Lulu's coat on her.

"Why is she coming?" I ask.

"Ava needs a break," Dad says.

So what? I think. *I need a break from Lulu too.*

So Lulu comes with us to the park. The football Dad has brought is pink. It has princesses on it. It is a Lulu ball.

"It's too small," I say.

Dad just looks at me. Is he thick? He doesn't seem to get it.

"The ball. It's too small," I say. "And it's pink."

"So?" Dad says. "We can still play."

He starts playing football with Lulu. Lulu laughs and tries to catch it.

"Dad! Dad!" I say. "To me!"

Dad holds Lulu's hand. Then he kicks the ball to me. Lulu runs towards it. I go to kick the ball back.

"Watch out!" Dad says. "Mind Lulu."

Lulu wobbles and giggles.

"You love this, don't you, Lulu?" Dad says.

"We can't play football with Lulu here," I say.

"'Course we can," says Dad.

I groan. He really, *really* doesn't get it.

We carry on. But Lulu is always in the way. It's not proper football. It's Lulu football. Pathetic!

The ball spins towards me. I kick it hard. It takes off. And hits Lulu in the face. Smack!

"Jeza!" Dad yells.

Lulu falls backwards. It goes quiet. Then she starts to scream. And scream. And scream.

Dad runs and picks Lulu up. There is a smear of blood on Lulu's face. I feel terrible. I stare at them. Dad is cuddling Lulu. She won't stop crying.

"What the hell have you done?" Dad yells at me. Lulu is still wailing.

"Well, if Lulu hadn't been here it wouldn't have happened!" I scream.

"You kicked the ball at her! You hurt her!" Dad shouts.

"Shut up!" I yell back. "It was an accident!"

And I run. I don't know where I am going.
But I still run.

I run until I can't breathe. I have no idea
where I am going. I don't live round here. I
don't know the places here. Not properly.
There are no cars. No people.

I am next to a canal, near a bridge.

I stop under the bridge and lean on it. I
feel like my head is going to burst, I'm so
angry.

There's an empty can. I kick it. Hard
against the wall. It bounces off and into the
canal.

There's a splash as it hits the water.

There is an old trolley nearby. A supermarket one. It's all manky and mashed up. I kick that too.

My foot hurts. But I don't care. I kick the trolley again and again, until it lands in the canal.

The water flies up in the air as the trolley hits it. Then the trolley sinks.

I can't see it any more.

I look around but the canal side is empty and I am alone.

Chapter 5

The Talk

I stand there for a while. I don't know how long for. I can hear my breath. I'm still feeling angry. But then I start to feel a bit of an idiot.

I try to remember how I got here.

I look round. I walk back to the park. Then I see a road I know. I run to the bus stop. I want to go back to Mum. I can feel an old woman staring at me as I wait at the stop. Tears are stinging in my eyes. But I won't let them fall. I hate Dad.

The bus doesn't come. But Dad does. Without Lulu.

"You all right, Jeza?" he asks.

I don't answer. I wish the bus would come.

"We need to talk," says Dad.

"Huh!" I say.

"Come on," says Dad. "Let's go for a burger."

I say nothing.

"Please?" asks Dad.

If the bus was here, I'd get on.

"Come on, Jeza – let's get a burger," Dad says again.

The old woman stares at us.

"Please?" says Dad.

I look at my feet. I say nothing for ages. The old lady shakes her head and tuts.

I don't know her. But she makes me feel like I'm being an idiot. I must look stupid.

"Oh, all right," I say.

I walk off in front of Dad. But I have no idea where the burger bar is.

"This way," says Dad.

And I follow on behind.

We get our burgers and take them to a table.

"What was that all about?" Dad asks. "All that in the park?"

He hasn't got a clue what I did at the canal. I don't suppose he would care. I glare at him.

"You just don't get it do you?" I sulk.

"Get what?" Dad says. "You hurt Lulu. What's wrong with you?"

"Nothing's wrong with *me*," I tell him.

Then I tell him that all he cares about is Lulu. And Fliss. And he doesn't even see her any more. He doesn't care about me at all.

He doesn't know anything about my mates. Or how I'm doing at school. Or football. Even when he does ask me about my life, he doesn't listen to what I say.

"You don't even come to see me play at matches," I finish. "All the other dads come. I just have Mum."

As soon as I say it, I feel bad. Not for Dad, but for Mum. I don't want Dad to think that I don't care about Mum.

"You never spend any time with me," I go on.

"I'm here with you now, aren't I?" Dad says.

"Only because Lulu got hurt," I reply.

"That's not true," says Dad.

And then he tells me he didn't realise that I missed him so much. He thought I didn't want to spend much time with him.

Well, he got that wrong, didn't he?

Chapter 6

Bad Brother

Dad gets me to go back to his house. Ava glares at me. Lulu's got a bruise on her cheek. Her eyes are red with tears. I feel bad. I wish I hadn't hit her with the ball.

"Jeza!" Lulu says. She's grabbed Ava's leg. She points at me but doesn't come over.

She hides her head in Ava's trousers.

Ava says nothing. She looks like she wants to yell at me.

"Hey, Lulu," I say. "You OK?"

Lulu looks at me and nods.

"Jeza play?" she asks.

"Sure," I say.

At least playing with Lulu will get me out of Ava's way. Ava is looking at me like she wishes I would disappear and never come back.

Lulu jigs up and down. It's like I've done the best thing in the world, when all I've said is that I will play with her.

Lulu runs over and grabs my hand.

"Jeza play! Jeza play!" she says and pulls me to her toy box.

We spend the afternoon playing bricks and trains. Ava spends the afternoon watching me like a hawk. Like she doesn't trust me not to hurt Lulu again.

It's a pretty boring weekend. We go to a car boot sale on Sunday morning. Dad buys me a PS3 game. It's not new but the bloke says it works. I'll have a go on it when I get home.

Later, Dad walks with me to the bus stop. He waits there with me.

"I've got a match this week," I say.

"My school's playing the Academy team at home."

"That's good," says Dad.

"It's on Wednesday," I say. "You could come?"

The bus pulls up.

"I'll have to see," says Dad. "Take care of yourself, Jeza."

"You too," I say.

I show my ticket and sit down. The bus pulls off.

Chapter 7

A Load of Rubbish

When I get home, Grandpa is there.

"Good weekend?" he asks.

"Yeah," I say, not looking him in the eye.

I don't want to tell him what really
happened. I don't want to tell anyone.

"Where's Fliss?" I ask.

"Up in her room. Revising," says Mum.

"I'll just finish my tea," says Grandpa.
"Then I'll help you put the rubbish out, Jeza."

The rubbish is taken away on Mondays.
And Grandpa thinks getting it ready is another
job that only men should do.

"It's OK. I've got some homework to do,"
I say. "I'll do it later."

"Let's just do it now," says Grandpa. He
stands up. "Otherwise you might forget. And
your mum needs you to help. You are the man
about the house, after all."

Why would I forget? I always do it.
Every week.

"What's your problem?" I ask. "Why do you always get at me? Why can't Fliss do it?"

"Fliss is revising," says Grandpa.

"Huh!" I spit. "So she can be clever and I can sort the rubbish out! Thanks, Grandpa!"

"Jeza!" Mum snaps at me. "Don't talk to Grandpa like that!"

I can feel my cheeks burning. Grandpa's mouth is open. He looks shocked.

"Why can't you just give me a break?" I shout back.

I grab the kitchen bin and pull out the bag of old tea bags and other slimy stuff. It stinks. I storm down the hall with it, open the front door and toss the bag of rubbish into the bin.

Then I drag the bin to the gate. Loudly.
Scraping it across the pavement.

I turn round to go back in the house.
Grandpa is in the hall. He is putting his coat
on.

"I'll be off, then," he says. He even tries
to smile at me. As if nothing has happened.

"Bye, Jeza," he says.

"Bye," I mumble.

I want to say sorry to Grandpa. I know
I was rude to him. But I can't get the words
out. I push past him and go up to my room.
Mum calls me. But I ignore her. And after a
bit, she stops calling.

Chapter 8

The Match

It's a boring week at school. The only good thing is that there is a fire alarm during maths. So we miss most of the lesson.

On Wednesday, it's the match. It's straight after school and we are playing on our pitch. Rory, Kismat, Callum and me are excited.

We need to win this match to stay in the league. We think we can do it.

We leave the changing rooms. Parents are standing around the edge of the pitch. I look out to see Dad. But he's not there.

The game starts. We play well. At half time it's one all. I look for Dad again, but there is no sign of him.

I should have sent him a text last night. To remind him. *Again*.

We talk tactics with our teacher.

"We can win this," he says. "Come on, boys!"

Play starts again. Rory scores the second goal. Then Callum another one. We are two up. It feels good.

I look over to the side of the pitch. All the dads are cheering. Calling out their sons' names. But my dad still isn't there. There's no one to cheer for me.

It's almost the end of the game when I hear a voice I recognise, urging me on as I get possession of the ball.

It's Mum.

Then the whistle goes. Game over. We've won! It feels brilliant.

"That was great, Jeza!" says Mum when I come out of the changing room.

"I thought Dad was going to come," I say.

"Oh, did you?" She looks at me. "Well never mind. I came," she says.

I throw my kit bag down on the pavement at the bus stop.

"It's not the same," I sulk, and shove my hands in my coat pockets.

"Well, I'm sorry," says Mum. She's cross now. "Perhaps I shouldn't have come. And I rushed here straight from work as well."

Now I feel bad. I know Mum came straight from work. I know Mum tries to come to all my matches, even though she doesn't really get football.

Dad loves football. Which makes it even worse that he never came.

We go home in silence. At least Mum doesn't nag on about stuff. She tells Fliss all about our win when we get home.

"Oh wow, how *amazing*," says Fliss. She is *so* not bothered. She doesn't even look up from the telly.

Mum doesn't say anything about Dad not coming. Or about me being rude.

I check my phone to see if Dad has sent me a text. Nothing. There isn't a message on the home phone either. Dad didn't come to the match and he hasn't even said why.

He'll contact me later. I'm sure he will. He said it would be good to see me playing football.

I do my homework. But I still haven't heard from Dad. I watch the telly. No text from Dad. I play the PS3 game Dad gave me and all my mates join in online.

Mum calls from downstairs. I have to stop
playing, because she doesn't like me sitting
on the computer all night. Five minutes later I
log off. Still no text from Dad. So I text him:

**Where were u? Why didn't u
come 2 footie?**

I wait. There's no reply.

I go downstairs and Mum is watching the
telly with Fliss.

"*Indiana Jones* is on in a minute," says
Mum. "Fancy watching that?"

I've seen it hundreds of times. But it's
still a good film.

"No way!" says Fliss. "There's Corrie on the other side."

"Well, I fancy *Indiana Jones*," says Mum. She winks at me. "I'll make some popcorn and it'll be just like the cinema."

Much later, the film is over. The popcorn bowl is empty. It's time for bed.

I get into the bathroom before Fliss and she has yet another strop.

"He'll be quicker than you are," says Mum.

"Only because he doesn't wash properly," says Fliss.

"I do!" I say as I brush my teeth. For longer than usual. Just to annoy her.

"Night, love," says Mum when I come out of the bathroom and Fliss storms in.

I check my phone. Still nothing. Maybe Dad didn't get my last text or something? Just in case, I text him again:

Did u get my last text?
Why didn't u come?

I stare at my phone. But the screen goes dim. No reply.

Chapter 9

Family Matters

Next day, after school, I am standing in the kitchen with Grandpa. He hasn't said anything about Sunday night. I want to say something, but I can't find the words.

"Good week at school, Jeza?" he says.

"Yeah," I reply. And I tell him about the football match. I don't mention Dad not coming. Then I tell Grandpa about the teacher at school called Mr Pool. He's got a car with the number plate **POOL 1**. The kids at school keep changing it to **POO 1** by sticking masking tape over the **L**. Mrs South, our head teacher, goes mental about it.

Grandpa laughs. Then he tells me about some of the things he did when he was my age. Like shooting a water pistol at the lady next door's washing. Lame stuff really. But we have a laugh.

"Mum's asked me to fix the washer on the kitchen tap," says Grandpa. "Want to help?"

I know that Mum has asked Grandpa round to make us be friends again. I also know that the tap really is dripping.

"Sure, Grandpa," I say.

And he teaches me how to repair the tap. It's quite cool. I wonder if Dad knows how to fix a tap. I've never seen him fix one.

"You know, I didn't really know my dad," says Grandpa.

I look at him. I've never heard this before. But then I've never talked to Grandpa about his dad before.

"He died when I was seven," Grandpa says.

"Died?" I say. I'm shocked. I had no idea. "What did he die of?"

"Heart attack," says Grandpa. "And I wasn't allowed to go to his funeral. My mum thought I was too young. I wasn't allowed to see him in hospital either. It was like my dad just disappeared."

Grandpa looks sad. He sits there thinking, saying nothing.

"I'm really sorry, Grandpa," I say. "I never knew that."

We talk about it for a while. How Grandpa learned to do all the jobs his dad had once done because he wanted to help his mum. How he missed his dad.

Then Fliss and Mum come back and the kitchen is full of noise again.

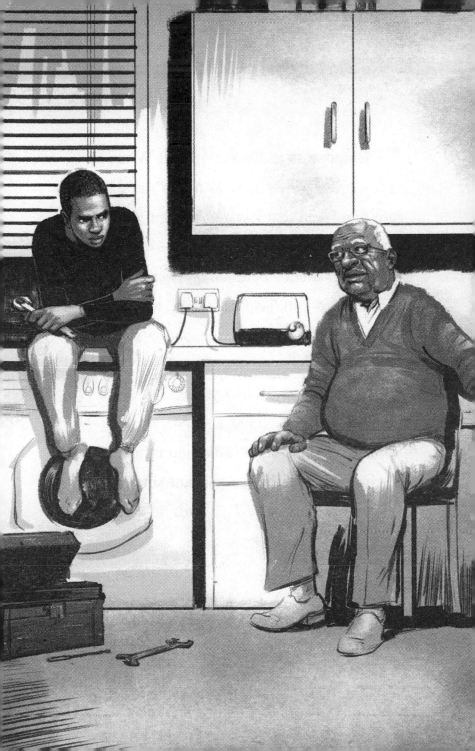

Grandpa stays to eat with us. When he goes, I give him a hug. I know I'm lucky I've got him. And that I've got my dad. I may not see much of him, but at least he's still around.

Later, when I'm alone, I check my phone again. Dad still hasn't bothered to text me back. I feel a surge of rage, and write:

I hate you!

I go to press send. But then I think about Grandpa and his dad. I press delete instead.

Chapter 10

The Reply

It's Friday and I am on my way back from school. My phone beeps. It's a text.

Couldn't get to match – sorry.
Was busy at work. Dad

I can't believe that's *all* he has to say. And that it took him *two days* to reply. I press delete. I'm so angry I want to throw my phone on the pavement. But I don't. I stuff it back in my pocket and storm off down the street.

If all the other dads made it to the match, my dad could have. Couldn't he? Then I think. Perhaps he really did have to work? But why didn't he tell me before? Why didn't he at least text me?

I get my phone out. I text back:

I want to see you! Now? Where?

Dad texts back straight away.

Can't – at work. Tomorrow?
Meet you in town at 11?

I text him back and say yes.

Dad is already in town when I get there. We
go to a café. We both have hot chocolate with
loads of cream on top.

"Sorry about the football," Dad says.
"How did it go?"

I look at him. Why should I tell him? He
could have come. He would have seen for
himself. Like the other dads.

Dad looks at me.

"Jeza?" he asks. "How did the game go?"

"You didn't come," I say.

Dad looks down at his hot chocolate. He doesn't say anything.

"You never come and see me play," I say.

"I was busy," he says. "I had to work."

"Mum's busy," I say. "She's always busy. And she works too. But she came."

Dad shifts in his seat. He goes to say something. But he stops.

"You didn't even answer my text," I moan. "Why don't you ever want to spend time with me?"

"I do! I am now, aren't I?" he says. He sounds cross. But I don't care.

"Like, for the first time in ages," I reply. "You spend loads of time with Lulu."

Dad looks at me.

"Well, I live with Lulu," he says.

"Exactly!" I say. "I hardly ever see you. And when I do, I can't talk to you."

"It's not like that, Jeza...," starts Dad.

"It *is* like that!" I shout. My voice is too loud. But it's like I can't control it. "All you ever do is play with Lulu, or ask me about Fliss. I hate it!"

"Jeza!" Dad snaps.

People in the café turn round. Why are people always staring at me? I can feel my cheeks going red.

"You see Lulu all the time!" I yell.

"And if you want to know what's going on with Fliss, ask her yourself!"

Dad looks angry. And then he looks sad.

"I know," he says quietly. "I wish I had more time to spend with you. With *all* of you."

I look at my hot chocolate. It has a skin on the top. It's disgusting. I don't look at Dad.

"But I've got time today," says Dad. "And I've bought these."

I look up. Dad is holding tickets. For a local football match.

"It's today," Dad says. "Want to come?"

I hesitate. Then I nod.

"Great," Dad says. "You'd better ring your mum and let her know."

Chapter 11

Time with Dad

It isn't a Championship match. Just the local team, who are in League One. But it is good. I've never been to a match with Dad before. I've only been to a proper game once, for Rory's birthday.

I see Callum there with his dad. We talk. Like it's normal for both of us to be at the footie with our dads.

Dad and I talk about the game on the bus home. We talk non-stop. We say how much better we'd have played if we had been on the pitch.

Dad says we could go back to his to eat. Lulu is mad with excitement when we go in.

"Jeza! Jeza!" she says.

She seems more pleased to see me than to see Dad. Ava gives me a look.

"Hi," I say.

I'm not going to say anything about last time I was there. I know I should say sorry.

But I don't know how to begin. So I say nothing.

Ava gives us pizza and she and Lulu have made a huge cake. I can tell Lulu helped make it. The icing is mad and wobbly. But it tastes great.

Later, Dad walks me to the bus stop.

"I had fun today," he says. "It's good to be just the lads."

I smile. I can't stop myself from smiling.

"Yeah," I say.

"We should do it again," says Dad. "I mean, I can't afford footie every week. But we could see that film. The one you wanted to see?"

"But you said Lulu couldn't go to it," I say.

"Well, she can't," says Dad. "But you and me can go and see it. Just the boys?"

I look at Dad.

"When?" I ask, hoping he really means it this time.

"I'll check with Ava and get back to you," says Dad.

Then the bus comes. I hug Dad and get on.

Chapter 12

Mum's Great Idea

The house is full of girls when I get home. Fliss has got her mates round for a sleepover. They're giggling at some film. They giggle at me too when they see me. I groan. Why are girls so dumb?

I go with Mum into the kitchen. She toasts me a sandwich.

"Those girls are stupid," I say. And I moan about them to Mum.

"Why don't you have some friends round?" Mum says. "You could have a lads night in?"

"But Fliss will just moan at us all the time," I say.

"Well she can go and stay with a friend for the night," Mum says. "Or stay at Dad's."

Nice one, I think. A house with no Fliss. No nagging. No shouting. No girls.

Well, I suppose there would be Mum. But she wouldn't count.

"We could get food in for your friends," Mum goes on. "And some DVDs."

"Or games," I say. "They'd be better. We're not babies."

"OK," Mum agrees.

Then Fliss comes in and Mum tells her about my mates coming over.

"I don't want loads of skanky boys in the house," says Fliss.

"Well, tough," says Mum. "You're having a sleepover. Next time it's Jeza's turn to have his friends round. If you don't want to be here, perhaps you could spend some time with your father?"

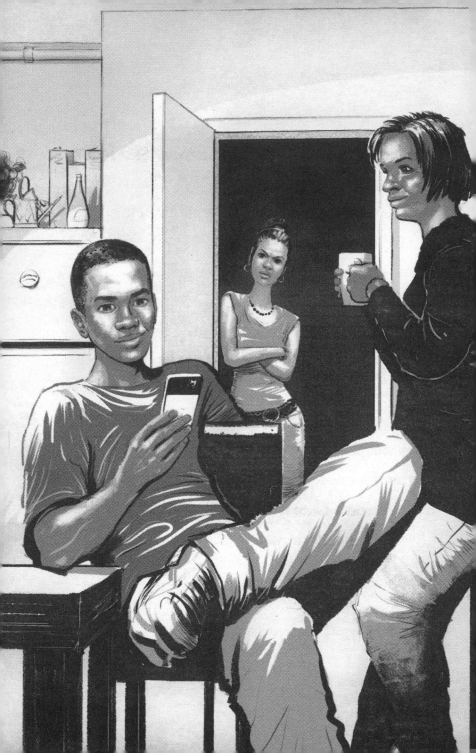

Fliss storms out of the kitchen. She goes back to her friends.

"Victory!" I say.

And me and Mum laugh.

Later, I get a text:

Today was good. See you soon? Dad

I type:

Yes. Thanks.

And I mean it.

I hope Dad means it too. Because today was a good day.